SC

For this story's journey, thanks to
Liz Bicknell, Jane Yolen, and the
Willard/Andrews and Korinek families.
C.L.S.

First published 2000 by Walker Books Ltd
87 Vauxhall Walk, London SE11 5HJ

2 4 6 8 10 9 7 5 3 1

This book has been typeset in Bernhard Modern.

Printed in Hong Kong

British Library Cataloguing in Publication Data
A catalogue record for this book is
available from the British Library.

ISBN 0-7445-5620-1

The Copper Tin Cup

Carole Lexa Schaefer

illustrated by
Stan Fellows

WALKER BOOKS
AND SUBSIDIARIES
LONDON • BOSTON • SYDNEY

Sammy Carl drinks cocoa
from his favourite cup, a cup
made of copper and tin.
It is a cup that cannot break.
The handle, which fits just
right in Sammy Carl's hand,
ends in a curlicue snail.

On one side of the cup,
just below the smooth worn
place on the rim, there are
two finely etched letters.
Sammy Carl traces
them with a finger.
"S for Sammy.
C for Carl," he says.
"My name, my cup."
And it is. But Sammy
Carl knows that the cup
was not always his.

When Sammy Carl's mama
was a little girl, she sipped
lemonade from it at parties
for her dolls in the garden
on summer afternoons.

Afterwards, she washed the
cup herself, then dried it
with a soft checked towel
until the letters gleamed.
"S for Samantha.
C for Caroline.
My name, my cup," she said.
And she was right.
But she knew that the cup
had not always been hers.

Before, it had belonged to her papa, Sammy Carl's grandpa. As a boy, he lifted it off its hook in the old blue cupboard and ran out to the barn with it in the morning.

He set it next to the milking pail
under Hedda the cow. Squirts
of warm milk splattered into
the copper tin cup. *Ping-ka-ting-plash*.
He rubbed drops of milk off
the letters.
"S for Sam.
C for Charles.
My name, my cup," he said.
And that was so.

But first the cup had belonged to Grandpa's big sister, Sammy Carl's great-aunt Serena. She drank precious fresh water from it during the long sea journey to the family's new home.

Before going to sleep each
night, she held the cup
close and read the letters
with her fingers in the dark.
"S for Serena.
C for Carlotta.
My name, my cup,"
she whispered.
And it was true.

S.C.

The cup was made for her by her parents, Sammy Carl's great-grandpapa Samuel and great-grandmama Carla.

After the cup cooled, Carla, an engraver, etched in the letters: S and C.

Samuel, a coppersmith, hammered bright copper into the curved cup shape. Then he lined it with a layer of hot melted tin.

They gave the cup to Serena for
their long journey.

S.C.

Serena Carlotta's cup.

Sam Charles's cup.

Samantha Caroline's cup.

Sammy Carl's cup.

A copper tin family cup.

Sammy Carl sits in the winter moonlight and traces the letters again. Mama sits down beside him. He looks at her, then at the cup.

"Want to taste my cocoa?" he says.

"Yes, please," she says, and takes a sip.

"Mmm, delicious."

"Yes," says Sammy Carl.

He takes a sip too.

"Cocoa tastes best in our cup."